LUMP LUMP
and the
BLANKET *of* DREAMS
Inspired by Navajo Culture and Folklore

by Gwen Jackson

Winter is coming, but the little black bear, Lump Lump, isn't ready to go to sleep! With the help of his mother, the wise Blue Bird, and his forest friends, Lump Lump gathers materials for Spider Woman to weave him a blanket of dreams. Inspired by Navajo/Diné culture and folklore, and featuring the work of famed weaver Barbara Teller Ornelas, this beautiful tale of family and friends takes the reader on a journey through the rich traditions and spectacular landscapes of the Southwest.

Gwen Jackson graduated magna cum laude from Lincoln University with a B.A. in psychology. She won a Ford Foundation Fellowship and attended the University of Michigan, where she received an M.A. in psychology.

An avid lover of history, anthropology, and people, Gwen has traveled to Canada, Mexico, the Caribbean, Spain, Portugal, Morocco, Sicily, Capri, the Greek Islands, Italy, Turkey, Israel, Jordan, Egypt, Singapore, Sri Lanka, the Philippines, Bali, Malaysia, Thailand, and India.

Gwen's main wish in life is Thurber's Dog Wish: "a strange and involved compulsion to be as happy and carefree as a dog."

Parents, Teachers, and Librarians

For more information on educational activities and presentations (language arts, social science, math, science, ESL, drama, art, Navajo weaving, and bears/hibernation) related to this book, go to

gwenjacksonstories.com

ONCE IN A forest was a fir tree. At the top of the fir tree was a little hole, and there lived Blue Bird. In the ground below the fir tree was a big hole, and there lived Blue Bird's best friends, Mother Bear and her little bear, Lump Lump.

At dawn, Blue Bird sang the colors of the forest through the morning mist, and she awakened each day with gladness:

> *Awake in beauty!*
> *Awake in beauty!*
> *Today we will live in beauty!*

After her busy days in the forest, Blue Bird told stories to Mother Bear and Lump Lump.

One night after Blue Bird told a story, Mother Bear said to Lump Lump, "Enjoy Blue Bird's stories while you can. Soon we will go to sleep for the winter."

Lump Lump stopped munching on his honeycomb. "Asleep for the winter? But I want to run in the forest. I want to eat more honey."

"Che-check," called Blue Bird. "Sleeping can be very nice, too."

"As nice as honey?" asked Lump Lump.

Blue Bird said, "Listen! I'll sing you a song about a blanket of dreams:

> *Now we will weave a blanket of dreams.*
> *May the white light of morning beautify this blanket.*
> *May the red light of evening beautify this blanket.*
> *May the falling rain beautify this blanket.*
> *May the rainbow beautify this blanket.*
> *May everyone sleep in beauty under a blanket of dreams.*
> *May everyone sleep in beauty!*
> *May everyone sleep in beauty!"*

"May I have a blanket of dreams?" asked Lump Lump.

"My, my," replied Mother Bear.

"Che-check," called Blue Bird.

"The blanket of dreams could keep us warm," mused Lump Lump. "I wouldn't mind sleeping all winter if I had a blanket of dreams."

"I KNOW MANY birds in the forest," observed Blue Bird, "who have flown across the mountains and the mesas, and across the fields and the forests of the Southwest. They have heard many stories. I am certain the birds can help us find a weaver."

"Really?" wondered Mother Bear. "And who could weave such a thing?"

"You get everything to make the blanket, and I'll get the net of twilight to hold it. Don't worry. We'll find a weaver," said Blue Bird.

Early the next morning, when Mother Bear and Lump Lump woke up, there was the net of twilight inside the den as Blue Bird had promised.

"Let's go see Robin," said Mother Bear, as she and Lump Lump walked toward the big rock.

"Oh, Robin, Robin," called Mother Bear.

Robin flew from her nest in the yellow pine tree to the big rock.

"Robin, could you get me the white light of morning for the blanket of dreams?" said Mother Bear.

"I don't know how," replied Robin.

"You're a good flyer," prompted Mother Bear. "I think you can do it."

Robin flew away, and Mother Bear said, "Come, Lump Lump. Let's gather grass for Robin's nest."

Later that morning, Robin returned with a piece of the white light of morning, and Mother Bear and Lump Lump gave her the grass they had gathered.

ALL THE WAY home, Lump Lump munched on his honeycomb and sang, "The white light of morning, the red light of evening, the falling rain, and the r-aa-iii-nnnnbow."

That evening, Mother Bear said, "Let's go see Hawk," as she and Lump Lump walked toward Hawk's aspen tree.

"Oh, Hawk, Hawk," called Mother Bear.

Hawk flew from his nest in the aspen tree.

"Hawk," asked Mother Bear, "could you get me the red light of evening for the blanket of dreams?"

"I don't know how," replied Hawk.

"You're a good hunter," encouraged Mother Bear. "I think you can do it."

Hawk flew away, and Mother Bear said, "Come, Lump Lump. Let's gather leaves for Hawk's nest."

Later that evening, Hawk returned with a piece of the red light of evening, and Mother Bear and Lump Lump gave Hawk the leaves they had gathered.

All the way home, Lump Lump munched on his honeycomb and sang, "The white light of morning, the red light of evening, the falling rain, and the r-aa-iii-nnnnbow."

Now that they had gathered the white light of morning and the red light of evening, Mother Bear and Lump Lump had to wait until it rained so they could catch the falling rain. But each morning when Lump Lump poked his head out of the den, the ground was spotted with early light. And each night after Blue Bird finished telling stories and Lump Lump lay nice and snug next to Mother Bear in the den, all he heard was the click-click of the branches and the soft rustle of the autumn leaves.

THEN ONE NIGHT just as Lump Lump started to dream about a giant honeycomb, he heard, "phlaaatt, phlaaatt, phlaaatt."

"It's raining!" cried Lump Lump, looking out of the den. "May I take the net of twilight outside and catch the rain?" he begged.

"Be careful," said Mother Bear.

Lump Lump lifted the net of twilight and went outside and held it open – and in fell the rain.

Whoosh! Blue Bird's tiny feathers almost tickled Lump Lump's nose as she flew to the ground.

"Che-check," greeted Blue Bird. "Now all we need for the blanket of dreams is to find the rainbow and a weaver."

"The white light of morning, the red light of evening, the falling rain, and the r-aa-iii-nnnnbow," sang Lump Lump.

"And the r-aa-iii-nnnnbow," sang Blue Bird.

Mother Bear poked her head out of the den. "Hush now, and come back in the den, Lump Lump," she scolded. "You'll wake up all the animals in the forest with that noise."

Now that Lump Lump had caught the falling rain, he could not rest until he found the rainbow. He poked his head into every hole. He climbed trees. He groped under bushes.

"Really? Lump Lump," sighed Mother Bear. "I keep telling you a rainbow is in the sky."

"ALWAYS IN THE sky?" asked Lump Lump, shaking a bush he hadn't explored.

"Always." Mother Bear patted Lump Lump's head. "And the r-aa-iii-nnnnbow," she sang.

But Lump Lump was so tired of waiting and so eager to search, he could not be cheered up or calmed down. So he ran off to grope under a juniper bush.

Then one day when Mother Bear and Lump Lump were walking by the stream, Mother Bear said, "Look...."

"A rainbow," whispered Lump Lump. He was so excited he dropped his honeycomb.

Just then Fox came by.

"Fox," asked Mother Bear, "could you get me a piece of the rainbow for the blanket of dreams?"

"I don't know how," replied Fox.

"You're clever," praised Mother Bear. "I think you can do it."

Fox crept into the stream and started walking toward the rainbow, and Mother Bear said, "Come, Lump Lump. Let's dig a den for Fox."

Later that afternoon, Fox returned with a piece of the rainbow, and Mother Bear and Lump Lump showed him the den they had dug.

11

ALL THE WAY home, Lump Lump munched on his honeycomb and sang, "The white light of morning, the red light of evening, the falling rain, and the r-aa-iii-nnnnbow."

The next day, Lump Lump sat in the den munching on a honeycomb when – whoosh! – Blue Bird flew into the den, almost tickling Lump Lump's nose with her tiny feathers.

"Che-check," greeted Blue Bird. "Spider Woman is living in the forest and she said she will weave the blanket of dreams."

"My, my," said Mother Bear. "You're a smart bird."

"Spider Woman?" said Lump Lump.

"Spider Woman," explained Blue Bird, "is the one who taught the Navajos/Dine´, the best weavers, how to weave. She's staying at the end of the forest, but she will be here for only one more day before she goes on a long walk in the desert. We must bring her presents for weaving the blanket of dreams." Blue Bird flapped her tiny wings.

"We will gather the best herbs," said Mother Bear.

"And I will give her a honeycomb," decided Lump Lump, looking worriedly at his stash of honey.

"Lump Lump," urged Mother Bear, "we must rush, so you stay here until we return. We don't have time for bears who sing or poke their noses in bushes."

LUMP LUMP CHOSE a big honeycomb for Spider Woman and sat down to wait for Mother Bear and Blue Bird. But each minute seemed to last forever, and he took a little nibble of honeycomb and then another little nibble, and when Mother Bear and Blue Bird returned to the den to get the net of twilight, he was so excited he bounded out of the den, forgetting he'd nibbled away Spider Woman's honeycomb.

After Mother Bear, Lump Lump and Blue Bird had gone past the big rock and by the stream to the end of the forest, they saw a loom made of tree trunks, and Spider Woman sat in front of the loom.

"Che-check," Blue Bird called. "We are honored that you will weave a blanket of dreams for us."

"Here are the finest herbs," said Mother Bear, "as a gift to you."

Mother Bear looked at Lump Lump. Lump Lump looked at his sticky paw.

"Is that the net of twilight?" asked Spider Woman. "I need to work quickly so that I can finish Lump Lump's blanket. Come, let me see you, Lump Lump."

Very slowly, as if he had rocks in his paws, Lump Lump walked up to Spider Woman.

"I think you're a kind bear to give gifts to Robin, Hawk, and Fox," said Spider Woman.

As Spider Woman looked at Lump Lump, her eyes told stories, and Lump Lump regretted he hadn't brought her any honey.

Spider Woman picked up a ball of yarn and took the white light of morning out of the net of twilight and began to weave. And as she weaved, she sang a song so beautiful no one could move and no one could speak, for the song came not just from Spider Woman, but from the wind in the trees and the breath in their hearts.

Yet Lump Lump thought, "I must give Spider Woman a gift," and he crept away from Mother Bear and ran by the stream and past the big rock to his den.

"Bears!" called Lump Lump. "I need you to help me carry my honey – all my honey – to Spider Woman."

All the forest bears filed into Lump Lump's den and each took a honeycomb, and then they all ran behind Lump Lump past the big rock and by the stream to Spider Woman's loom. Each bear laid a honeycomb into the basket, until soon, a mound of honeycombs shone like gold. When the last bear laid the last honeycomb on the mound, Spider Woman stopped weaving.

"The blanket of dreams is finished," she said. "Do you like it?"

"My, my," marvelled Mother Bear.

"Che-check," called Blue Bird, flapping her tiny wings. "The blanket of dreams is too beautiful for words."

"Is that honey for me?" asked Spider Woman.

"That's all my honey," answered Lump Lump, "and it's all for you."

Now, as Lump Lump looked at Spider Woman, he saw the mountains and the mesas and the fields and the forests of the Southwest.

"May you sleep in beauty," said Spider Woman.

After Mother Bear, Lump Lump and Blue Bird had gone by the stream and past the big rock and were back in the den, Mother Bear remarked, "There's cold in the air. It's bear-sleeping weather now."

"Are you sleepy, Lump Lump?" she said.

Lump Lump's head felt heavy, like a big rock. "Could I hear a story?" he yawned.

"And the r-aa-iii-nnnbow," sang Mother Bear, tucking the blanket of dreams nice and snug across Lump Lump.

"Che-check," called Blue Bird. "Stories are nice, but sleeping can be very nice, too."

17

WITH HER TINY beak, Blue Bird pushed the last corner of the blanket of dreams nice and snug against Lump Lump.

"You know, Blue Bird," said Mother Bear, "I know a bear, a very kind bear, who is a very singing bear and a very poking-his-nose-in-the-bushes bear who gave his honey to Spider Woman."

"All his honey," said Lump Lump. "And you know what?" he said, his voice thick with sleep. "He's sharing the blanket of dreams with Blue Bird in the spring so she can dream new stories."

Blue Bird bowed her tiny head and flapped her wings – whoosh! – almost tickling Lump Lump's nose.

"What a kind bear!" praised Mother Bear, and she licked Lump Lump twice, and patted him on the head with her paw.

"Are you going away for the winter?" Mother Bear asked Blue Bird, and Blue Bird sang:

> *Tomorrow I will fly away in gladness.*
> *Tomorrow I will fly away in beauty.*
> *And when I think of you, my friends,*
> *My tiny heart shall beat in beauty.*
> *Sleep in beauty!*
> *Sleep in beauty!*

"Che-check," called Blue Bird before she flew out of the den.

Outside the den, a cold wind blew, and Lump Lump heard Spider Woman's song in the wind and in the warm breath of his heart. He snuggled close against Mother Bear and was soon fast asleep, and so was Mother Bear.

Throughout the long winter, while snow whitened the forest and cold mists blew through the pine trees, Mother Bear and Lump Lump lay sleeping in the den. Nice and snug under the blanket of dreams, they did not feel cold or lonely, for the blanket of dreams was also a blanket of love....

I DEDICATE THIS BOOK WITH LOVE AND GRATITUDE TO MY MOTHER, JANET HARMON.

Contributor: Barbara Teller Ornelas, sixth generation Navajo weaver. Her weavings are displayed in the Smithsonian Museum, the British Museum, and many other galleries. She graciously allowed me to use her weaving, Child's Blanket, for the blanket of dreams. She also gave advice on the story and the pictures. More information on Navajo weavings is available at navajorugweavers.com.

Contributors: Darrell and Lorna Smith, long-time biologists and large carnivore specialists. Lorna is Executive Director for the non-profit organization Western Wildlife Outreach (WWO). Darrell is a wildlife biologist and science advisor to the organization. For information about bears such as Lump Lump and other large carnivores, WWO's website is Bearinfo.org or Western Wildlife.org.

I extend my heartfelt gratitude to Dr. Paul Apodaca, Associate Professor of Sociology and American Studies at Chapman University, for informing me about Navajo culture and folklore.

I gratefully acknowledge the Tewa Pueblo prayer, "Song of the Sky Loom," which was the model for my Blanket of Dreams poem.

Thanks, also, to Cathy Notarnicola, Curator, Museum of Indian Arts and Culture, for kindly introducing me to Barbara Teller Ornelas.

And thanks to my dear friend, Adrienne Patel (of Adrienne Patel Fine Art), for her comments on the artwork.

21

◆ FriesenPress

Suite 300 - 990 Fort St
Victoria, BC, V8V 3K2
Canada

www.friesenpress.com

ISBN
978-1-4602-9929-6 (Hardcover)
978-1-4602-6438-6 (Paperback)
978-1-4602-6439-3 (eBook)

1. JUVENILE FICTION, FAIRY TALES & FOLKLORE, ADAPTATIONS

*1. Bears folklore - Fiction 2. Navajo Indian folklore -Fiction 3. Hibernation
- Fiction 4. Navajo weaving -Fiction 5. Bedtime stories- Fiction
6.Native American folklore -Fiction 7. Friendship - Fiction*

Distributed to the trade by The Ingram Book Company

Summary: A little black bear and his forest friends gather materials for Spider Woman, a holy woman
in Navajo/Dine' culture and folklore, to weave a blanket of dreams for his winter's hibernation.

CPSIA information can be obtained at www.ICGtesting.com
Printed in the USA
LVIW01n1459140917
548742LV00007B/99